Swing, Otto, Swing!

SIMON SPOTLIGHT
An imprint of Simon & Schuster Children's Publishing Division
1230 Avenue of the Americas, New York, New York 10020
This Simon Spotlight edition September 2017
Copyright © 2004 by David Milgrim
SIMON SPOTLIGHT, READY-TO-READ, and colophon are registered trademarks of
Simon & Schuster, Inc.
For information about special discounts for bulk purchases,
please contact Simon & Schuster Special Sales
at 1-866-506-1949 or business@simonandschuster.com.
Manufactuerd in China 0118 SDI

The adventures of otto

Swing,
Otto,
Swing!

David Milgrim

Ready-to-Read

Simon Spotlight

New York   London   Toronto   Sydney   New Delhi

FOR
Wyatt

See Flip.

See Flip swing.

See Flop.

See Flop swing.

See Otto.

See Otto swing.

Hello, Otto.

Good-bye, Otto.

See Flip
give Otto
some tips.

See Otto try again.

See Flip and Flop
give Otto more tips.

See Otto learn.
Learn, Otto, learn.

See Otto swing . . .

See Otto saw.
Saw, saw, saw.

See Otto tie.
Tie, tie, tie.

See Otto swing.
Swing, Otto, swing!

The adventures of otto

See Santa Nap

David Milgrim

Ready-to-Read

Simon Spotlight

New York   London   Toronto   Sydney   New Delhi

For Lenny, Karina,
Celia, and Marc

SIMON SPOTLIGHT
An imprint of Simon & Schuster Children's Publishing Division
1230 Avenue of the Americas, New York, New York 10020
This Simon Spotlight edition September 2017
Copyright © 2004 by David Milgrim
For information about special discounts for bulk purchases, please contact
Simon & Schuster Special Sales at 1-866-506-1949 or business@simonandschuster.com.
Manufactured in China 0118 SDI

See Santa.
See Santa give.

Give, Santa, give.

Now Santa is all done.

See Santa nap.

Nap, Santa, nap.

See Flop.
See Flop's new drum.

Thank you, Santa!

See Santa
nap again.

Look, Pip got a
new water gun!
Thank you, Santa!

See Santa nap
one more time.

Look, Wally got
a new ball!
Thank you, Santa!

See Santa nap at last.

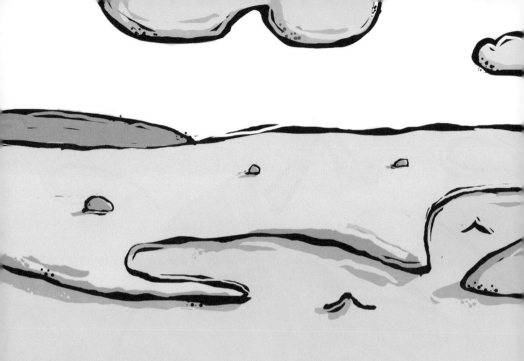

See Peanut.
See Peanut's new swimsuit.
Look out, Santa!

Uh-oh, there goes Santa!

See Santa get
no rest at all.

Look, Otto got a fishing pole!
Go, Otto, go!

See Otto save Santa!
Yay, Otto!

Uh-oh, where is Santa going now?

Look, Santa is in
Otto's tree house!
Thank you, Otto.

See Santa nap.

Nap, Santa, nap.

Ride, Otto, Ride!

For the real Otto

SIMON SPOTLIGHT
An imprint of Simon & Schuster Children's Publishing Division
1230 Avenue of the Americas, New York, New York 10020
This Simon Spotlight edition September 2017
Copyright © 2002 by David Milgrim
SIMON SPOTLIGHT, READY-TO-READ, and colophon are registered trademarks of
Simon & Schuster, Inc.
For information about special discounts for bulk purchases, please contact
Simon & Schuster Special Sales at 1-866-506-1949
or business@simonandschuster.com.
Manufactured in China 0118 SDI

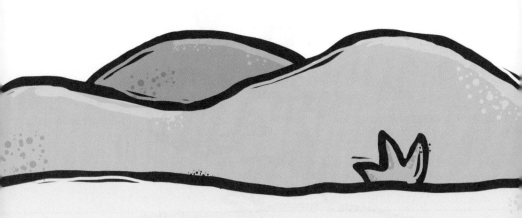

The adventures of otto

Ride, Otto, Ride!

David Milgrim

Ready-to-Read

Simon Spotlight

New York   London   Toronto   Sydney   New Delhi

See Flip and Flop.

See Flip and Flop walk.

Walk, Flip and Flop, walk.

Walk, walk, walk,
walk, walk.

See Flip huff.

See Flop puff.

Look! Here come
Peanut and Otto.

See Flip and Flop ride.

Ride, Flip and Flop, ride.

Look, there is Skip.

See Skip ride.

See Flip and Flop ride.

See Otto ride.

Ride, everyone, ride.

Look, here are
Al, Sal, Hal, and Val.
Hop on up!

See Peanut go.
Go, Peanut, go.

Look, there is Spec.

See Spec hop on too.

See Otto bang.

Bang, bang, bang!

See Peanut ride.
Ride, Peanut, ride!

The adventures of otto

Go, Otto, Go!

David
Milgrim

Ready-to-Read

Simon Spotlight

New York   London   Toronto   Sydney   New Delhi

SIMON SPOTLIGHT
An imprint of Simon & Schuster Children's Publishing Division
1230 Avenue of the Americas, New York, New York 10020
This Simon Spotlight edition September 2017

For information about special discounts for bulk purchases, please contact
Simon & Schuster Special Sales at 1-866-506-1949
or business@simonandschuster.com.
Manufactured in China 0118 SDI

See Otto.

See Otto look.

See Otto look
at his home.

See Otto work.

Work, Otto, work.

Work,

work,

work.

Look what
Otto made!

See Otto go.

See Otto go up.
Up, up, up.

Uh-oh.

See Otto go down.

Down,
down,
down.

See Otto
go here.

See Otto go there.

See Otto go . . . .

BAM

. . . nowhere.

See Otto.

See Otto look.

See Otto look at his home.

Home, sweet home!

See
Otto

The adventures of otto

See
Otto

David
Milgrim

Ready-to-Read

Simon Spotlight

New York   London   Toronto   Sydney   New Delhi

SIMON SPOTLIGHT
An imprint of Simon & Schuster Children's Publishing Division
1230 Avenue of the Americas, New York, New York 10020
This Simon Spotlight edition September 2017
Copyright © 2002 by David Milgrim
All rights reserved, including the right of reproduction in whole
or in part in any form.
SIMON SPOTLIGHT, READY-TO-READ, and colophon are registered
trademarks of Simon & Schuster, Inc.
For information about special discounts for bulk purchases, please contact
Simon & Schuster Special Sales at 1-866-506-1949
or business@simonandschuster.com.
Manufactured in China 0118 SDI

For Kyra

See Otto.

See Otto go.

Go,
Otto,
go!

Go, go, go.

Look, Otto is out of gas.

See Otto fall.

See Otto smile.

Smile, Otto, smile.

See
Otto
run.

Run,
Otto,
run.

See Otto fly.

Bye, Otto, bye.

See Flip.
See Flip paint.

See Flop.
See Flop sit.

Look, here comes Otto!

See paint fly.
Fly, paint, fly.

See everyone laugh.

Laugh, everyone, laugh.

See
Pip
Point

For Carole and Zane

SIMON SPOTLIGHT
An imprint of Simon & Schuster Children's Publishing Division
1230 Avenue of the Americas, New York, New York 10020
This Simon Spotlight edition September 2017
Copyright © 2003 by David Milgrim
All rights reserved, including the right of reproduction in whole or in part in any form.
SIMON SPOTLIGHT, READY-TO-READ, and colophon are registered trademarks of
Simon & Schuster, Inc.
For information about special discounts for bulk purchases, please contact
Simon & Schuster Special Sales at 1-866-506-1949
or business@simonandschuster.com.
Manufactured in China 0118 SDI

The adventures of otto

See Pip Point

David Milgrim

Ready-to-Read

Simon Spotlight

New York   London   Toronto   Sydney   New Delhi

See Pip.

See Pip point.

Point, point, point.
Point, point, point.
Point, point, point.

See Otto share.

Thank you, Otto.

Oops,
there goes Pip.

See Pip go.

Go, go, go.

Uh-oh.

See Pip go up.

See Pip go way up.

See Pip go up, up,
and away.

See Zee the Bee.

See Zee the Bee fly.

See Zee the Bee fly
in his sleep.

Look out, Zee!

See Pip go down.

See Pip go way down.

See Pip go down,
  down to the ground.

Look! Here comes Otto!
Hurry, Otto, hurry!

See Otto save Pip!
Thank you, Otto!

Uh-oh.

See Otto and Pip crash.

See Otto and Pip splash.

Oops.

See Pip point.